To the Tongva, First People of Los Angeles,
who once flourished in the sun,
and who gather there once more

And to spiritual truth seekers in every time

A prayer of thanks to the unnamed American Indians
whose graceful images
lend their heart and spirit to the illustrations.
I see you now
I see you in tomorrow

The name Tongva means "People of the Earth." The Tongva's ancestral homelands consisted of a massive section of Southern California encompassing the present Los Angeles basin, the San Fernando Valley to the north and much of Orange County to the south. Their territory also included the southern Channel Islands, including Santa Catalina, San Clemente and San Nicolas. These creative and spiritual people flourished in this warm, bountiful environment for thousands of years before the Spanish colonial explorers arrived in 1542.

In the northwestern reaches of the Tongva territory and in the coastal mountains, the chaparral-covered bluffs and ridges and the oak grasslands were home to many spirits who coexisted with the People and guided them. Others also came, now and then, from distant lands and times.

ONE

EYES CLOSED, TACU LAY ON HIS BACK ON THE
parched yellow grass of a steep, round hill beneath
the sacred peak known as *Asawtngna,* Place of the
Eagle. He was clothed only in a milkweed fiber belt
hung with his stone knife, and the early summer

sun burned into his light chestnut skin. Though the afternoon was peaceful, his thoughts whirled and crashed against each other like the breakers from the blue water that lay to the south, beyond the mountains.

Why must I lie here with my eyes closed, as defenseless as a field mouse within range of the red-tailed hawk? Like a deer hide stretched out to dry in the sun, I'll lie here until my spirit evaporates into the skies and I am no more! Why must I risk further humiliation like this—what if someone from the village comes and sees me? I am already in disgrace and have no friends left!

Tacu felt his pride and self-control wavering like the heated air rising at midday from the huge sandstone boulders near the village, *Tototngna*, the Place of the Stones. Hot moisture spread from under each closed eyelid and ran down his face in two streams. Mortified, he wiped his eyes and withdrew his thoughts, pulling them tightly around him as if they were the soft antelope-hides in which he had nestled as a small child. He drifted.

*An earlier time—the earliest. A flash of azure sky,
then the heady sensation of weightlessness and ecstasy,
and a gust of cool air. The dark moving silhouette
of his father, looking down at him with his piercing
golden gaze. Then he is enveloped in the pliant cradle
of his mother's mahogany arms. He laughs and reaches
his own arms back toward the sky.*

*Now his own strained voice, much more recent.
"Uncle, it is three years past the time for my initiation
ceremony. I am shunned even by very young boys who
have seen the grasses turn green only eleven and twelve
times! They have fasted in the sacred* Yobangnar
*enclosure and sought their first visions while I am
still known only by my childhood name. Yet I am old
enough to marry. If I cannot go to the village to learn
from the* Paha*—village religious chief—and seek
my spirit guide, I will never recover my dignity. No
woman will accept me as husband. Why do you forbid
me to go?"*

*"It is a worthy aim to learn such skills, to begin
a family and to become a competent member of your
community, Nephew. But from the time of your birth,
your path has been different from that of your people.*

11

I am here to show you that path. It is not so important what others say or think of you. Only concern yourself with your own actions."

The fierce sensation of burning spots all over his body brought Tacu to sudden painful consciousness. He leaped up. For an instant, his body appeared to be bleeding in countless tiny rivers. He swept his hands over his torso and saw that they were actually streams of biting red ants. As he brushed them off frantically, he felt himself observed and spun around to face uphill. Takoda, wearing his thong hunting belt and painted buckskin breechcloth, squatted in the yellow grass a short distance off, gazing at him impassively. Tacu blanched in embarrassment.

"Uncle, I did not realize I was to undergo this trial by pain. I could have prepared myself to endure! Now I have failed my test!"

"Your test was not that of enduring the bites of your little brothers, Nephew." Takoda stood. "You will come again tomorrow." He was gone.

In dismay and confusion, Tacu watched him leave, ignoring the fire again spreading over his feet and moving up his legs.

That evening, in their round, thatched reed *kich*—hut—Tacu lay on a hide and permitted his mother to tend to him. His legs and torso were covered with many small red welts.

"Why would my uncle place me in such a position? How can I do what is expected if I don't know what is to be done?"

Rómi carefully removed the pulp of boiled *avakhat*—cottonwood—leaves and bark from her mortar and spread them over his legs and torso. The poultice was soothing.

"You must trust him, for he has been our friend and guardian since before your father went east to dwell with the spirits. Your father honored him, and he has always helped us."

"Mother, I do honor my uncle, but I fear that these lessons are beyond me. I am too stupid to grasp them. I am filled with such frustration that I

only wish to leave and never come back!" He sighed. "And then I will never attain manhood or find a wife." Tacu shifted restlessly.

Rómi looked at him intently. "You must learn silence, to watch and listen. I have watched you as you have grown and I know that you are capable of learning your uncle's lessons. But if I tell you what he wants of you, the words will be empty and you will still lack understanding. Your uncle has many things to impart to you, and he must do it in his own way. This way will make you wiser."

Tacu mulled this over. His mother got to her feet and put the mortar away on a mat alongside the *kich* wall.

"Mother, where does my uncle go when the sun drops behind the western mountains?"

"He goes his own way. It is not for me to question him."

Tacu spoke hesitantly. "I mean no disrespect, Mother, but there is much about my uncle that arouses my curiosity. He is not of our people. He dresses his hair differently and he does not speak or move like the men in the village."

His mother took another hide from a corner and laid it out in preparation for sleep. "Since your observation is correct, I will explain it to you." She settled herself on the hide. "Your uncle comes from a northern land of wide plains bordered by very high mountains. His people revere their holy men, who have great wisdom and abilities. Your uncle is known by a name from the Lakota people, for he lived with them for a time. He came to our *kich* not long after you were born."

Tacu took this in. "I have dreamed of him. Though he comes to me in different shapes, I know it is him and though he doesn't speak, I know there is something he wants to tell me."

His mother gave him a wry look. "Never doubt that your uncle will tell you plainly everything he has a mind to, when he is sitting before you!"

"But this is different. Sometimes he is an eagle, sometimes a coyote. He also takes a human form that I do not recognize, in which he is dressed oddly—he wears loose leggings the color of burned wood that hang straight to his feet, and on his head is a stiff circular bonnet of dark brown hide. And

16

on his feet are the shiny shells of two huge black beetles!" Tacu looked sheepishly at his mother. "I can fathom no wisdom from these dreams."

Rómi smiled kindly. "Does not the dream suggest to you that your uncle has been given sacred power by the Giver-of-Life to be many things?"

Tacu's brow wrinkled in concentration. "Yes, that is true. It is good to find some meaning in my dreams. But why would he wear black beetle shells on his feet?"

Rómi made a soft scolding sound. "There is no need to trouble yourself unduly about your dreams. You will come to understand them at the proper time. Let us sleep now; you must arise early and resume your lesson."

Tacu sighed and went to spread out his sleeping hide.

TWO

NEXT MORNING, AS THE SUN WAS JUST LIFTING
into the eastern sky, Tacu lay again on the same
hill, struggling to keep his eyes closed. His skin
still itched from the ant bites, but he willed himself
to ignore it. Many thoughts competed for his

attention, foremost among them the unrelenting question of why he must lie here struggling to learn something he could not fathom. His only solace was the thought that here, in the steep foothills and mountains overlooking *Topangna*, near the northwestern borders of his people's great lands, none of the young men from the village were likely to surprise him. He couldn't have explained to them what he was doing here, lying on a hill with his eyes closed in a mysterious lesson that was not being supervised by the village *Paha*—religious leader—nor why he had failed to come to the village to participate in the initiation trials and ceremonies that all young boys did when they became men.

The harsh cry of a scrub jay brought him back to the present. He realized that he ought to remain vigilant to danger and to do so, he must stay alert. Since he didn't have the use of his eyes, he must listen for it. He could only do this if he kept his mind empty of thoughts. He lay and strained to hear all that was happening around him.

The only sounds were the distant drumming of woodpeckers on the oak trees, the rustle of the

wind in the dry yellow grasses around his body,
the cawing of crows, and the clicking and chittering
of insects. But as he lay and listened, fear began to
grow: the idea that something, perhaps *to-koó-ro't*—a
mountain lion—was crouching in the dry grass,
waiting to leap onto him. He heard the grass rustle in
the same place several times. He waited, tense, while
his fear grew into a conviction, and the conviction
grew until it was overwhelming. In one motion he
threw himself to his feet, letting out a wild cry and
pivoting rapidly, stone knife in hand, expecting to
find a hostile brave—or mountain lion—advancing on
him. He saw nothing. He scouted around the area,
checking the brush to see if something or someone
was retreating. But he found nothing out of the
ordinary; the grassland was as peaceful as it had been
when he first lay there. Sighing in annoyance at the
trick his mind had played on him, he returned to his
spot and lay down again.

It took him a short while to calm himself
and lie quietly alert again. But just when he finally
felt at peace with his surroundings, he felt an
insect land on his ankle. It began to crawl up his

leg. He tried to ignore it, but the harder he tried, the more acutely he was aware of the insect's tiny legs moving over his skin from side to side. Once above his knee, it deviated onto his inner thigh and crawled between his legs. Tacu's entire being became absorbed in resisting the tortuous tickling on his most sensitive skin. His uncle had instructed him to disregard small distractions; otherwise his mind, having won in tricking him into diverting his thoughts, would never stop bringing up further distractions. But this no longer felt like a small distraction, it absorbed all his attention.

A violent anger began to grow within him that this tiny creature should hold the power to so entirely dominate his attention as it toyed with him. He knew that he should be able to tolerate the sensation without flinching; nevertheless, his whole body quivered with the effort of holding still. He knew that in very few moments he would have to move.

He prayed silently: "*Y-yo-ha-riv-guina*—Giver-of-Life—I ask you to share with me your fortitude so that I may rise beyond this annoyance and prove

myself worthy. I mean no disrespect to your little brother, but he is making my task very difficult."

The answer came to him: *you should concentrate on something else.* He forced himself to listen to the distant tapping of a woodpecker and willed himself to focus on that sound alone. He could still feel the insect, but the sensation gradually diminished as he cast his attention away and listened. Gradually, as moments passed, among the intermittent sounds of the wind rustling the grass and birds he began to hear many other sounds, and he forgot about the crawling insect.

A very soft, swishing sound in the grass caught his attention. It continued, then grew fainter and died out. He realized it had been a snake gliding by. It must have been only a few arm-lengths away. Marveling at this, he then heard a minute scratching sound followed by a soft thud. Then a very faint whiffing sound. It was a ground squirrel peering out of its burrow. He realized the thud had been the squirrel dislodging a small lump of earth. The squirrel was only a short distance from Tacu, but unaware of his prone, still form.

Then he realized that he had not *heard* the dislodged piece of dirt fall, but *felt* its minute vibration when it hit the earth. It came to him that he had other means than sight and sound with which to sense his surroundings, and he became eager to find out what other sense messages he might discover. He willed himself to perceive every change in the earth and air around him.

Under the dry grasses crushed beneath his body, he felt with the skin of his back that the earth was actually moist and faintly cool with the dew that had formed during the night. The breeze that blew over him felt balmy and dry and the sun, now overhead, poured its heat onto him. He knew from the feeling of heat on his body that there were no clouds in the sky. With increasing elation, he felt as though he was reaching out to the land and air around him. A faint hoarse cry down the hill brought the mental image of a crow as it dropped from an oak branch to alight on the ground. The sound of the cry changed subtly as the crow moved from a higher position to the ground.

24

Then, with clarity, he realized that he innately knew exactly where he was—not only did he feel the size of his body compared to the hill on which he lay, but he sensed his position on the slope, a hundred paces down from the crest. From the rustling of leaves he knew the position of each of the life-nourishing oak trees that were scattered over the hill's rolling surface, and beyond that he was aware of the various crags and peaks that surrounded it. Though his eyes were still closed, he felt his presence in these surroundings as though he were standing looking at them. He had forgotten the distractions of his body and thoughts. He felt that nothing could creep upon him now without his knowing it.

With a rush of excitement, he realized that this was why Takoda had sent him here: he finally understood this lesson. He realized that his uncle was very wise to have set him this task.

He lay for a little while longer, at ease, yet feeling as tight and fit as a sinew bowstring just after the arrow has been released. It had grown cooler, and the sun through his eyelids had changed

its position. He opened his eyes. He saw that the sun was resting just above the ridge of mountains in the west, about to set. He felt a sense of wonder that he had been there the entire day. He rose to his feet and started home.

THREE

AS TACU BENT INTO THE LOW DOORWAY OF
his hut, he saw Takoda there with his mother, sitting behind the fire. Takoda's dark form flickered
as though he were made of smoke and orange
firelight. Tacu seated himself a little distance

from the fire, deferring to his elders. He was eager to tell his uncle about his day, but remained silent out of courtesy. His mother handed him his polished wood bowl, filled with acorn meal. She smiled at him, sensing his excitement.

Takoda regarded Tacu for some moments, then his black eyes softened in approval. "*Nachochan*—my eyes see your eyes, Nephew. How are you today?"

"*Tehépko é*—I am well, Uncle."

Tacu saw a newly emptied food bowl beside Takoda and knew he had already dined, so he began to eat.

"So, Nephew, tell me. What did you learn today?"

Tacu finished chewing a mouthful.

"Uncle, I heard and felt many things. I could sense things around me with my eyes closed, the same as if they had been open! And then I felt as large as the hill itself, and knew where all the animals, trees, and even the entire hill itself was." He hesitated. "Is this what you wanted me to see?"

"Yes, Nephew. You have done well."

Tacu's face brightened in pleasure.

Takoda continued. "Now listen: these perceptions, and the other things I will teach you, will stay with you always, if you remain true to yourself, your family, your people, and the spirits around you in the earth, sky, trees, mountains, and our relations, the animals."

Tacu's expression betrayed no emotion, but he didn't understand.

Takoda continued. "I speak of honesty, never lying nor accusing someone of lying unjustly. I speak of meeting challenges or danger and not backing down. If you observe a thing, do not say you saw another thing. If you give your opinion, do not change it to suit what you think another wants to hear. If you say you will do something, then do it. If you say you will not, then do not."

Takoda looked directly at Tacu. "All of these things are to say, never let fear govern your actions or cause you to fall back from action, if it is something you should do."

Tacu looked down. "Uncle, thoughts of fear cause me to avoid the village now." His voice

quavered. "I fear to encounter others younger than I who—who—" Tacu couldn't finish.

Takoda prompted him. "Tell me your concern. Fear not to speak."

Tacu let out all his breath in a burst. "I fear to meet boys younger than myself who have already been initiated. They consider me unworthy and think me a coward for not coming to the *Paha* for my initiation and to seek my vision. I cannot hold my head high in their presence. I am shamed."

Takoda considered Tacu's words. "You feel shame because you accept what they tell you. You accept when they accuse you of this misdeed, this cowardice. But doesn't shame come from one's own misdeed? What is your misdeed here, Nephew?"

"I haven't gone to the *Yobangnar,* as do all young men of my people who wish to enter manhood."

Takoda grunted, then reached into a pouch hanging at his belt and took out his carved soapstone pipe. He methodically filled it with tobacco from the pouch, then placed a burning coal from the fire on top of the tobacco and began puffing. Finally he spoke.

"Now attend to my words. It is an honor to study with the *Paha* and learn the spiritual knowledge of your people. But a young man must go only if he feels ready to enter manhood, not to please his comrades. Who are you trying to please, your comrades—your pride? Or are you ready to become a man and do all that a man must do, to counsel your people when needed, live as part of the community and contribute to its welfare while you care for a wife and children?"

Tacu looked sheepish. "I am ready to care for a wife and children!"

With a wry look, Takoda gestured with a hand in acknowledgment of what Tacu said. "It is good that you at least understand there is more to learn. One day, perhaps, you will become *tsinitsnits*—a wise man—if you study well."

Tacu looked at him, startled. "Uncle, it is not my wish to become a wise man. I merely wish to be able to take a wife and raise a family."

Takoda gazed at him impassively. "So, you don't want to be wise? I doubt that, Nephew. Be careful what you say you want or don't want. If you wish to be small or stupid, you will eventually

31

get your wish. While I am not the *Paha* of your village, I, too, in my travels, have learned a great deal and it is these things I want to impart to you before you go to the *Yobangnar* shelter to seek your initiation. I hope to rescue you from stupidity before age and your own foolishness bring it upon you. Now heed my words! Here is something else to remember. You need to learn to hold your position firmly in the face of any opposition, no matter whether you are a child or a village leader. Do you understand?"

Tacu nodded slowly. "Yes, Uncle."

"So it will be." Takoda reached into his pouch once more. "But now I have something to give you."

He extended his open hand to Tacu. In it lay a small, round, flat object the color of a pool of moonlit water, with the same shine. It was about the size of Tacu's large toenail. "Use this to remind you of the insights you gained today."

Tacu took the object from Takoda and examined it. He had never seen anything crafted as perfectly round as this disk. It was thin, shiny and hard, colder to the touch than shell or bone,

and of a glistening light material like the water under moonlight. But hardest to believe were the minute images carved into its faces. One side held the raised head of a brave in feathered headdress rendered as though he were real. In fact, it was so lifelike that he imagined it could be the spirit of a warrior somehow captured in this bright material.

Tacu looked up at Takoda with awe. "Uncle, this gift is like nothing I have ever seen." He turned the disk over. The other side held the figure of a grotesque creature that could either have been an insect like a flea or some huge beast—the size was uncertain.

"Uncle, what does this image depict?"

"That creature is the buffalo, a powerful spirit who owns the distant plains far to the north. He provides many gifts to my people who live there— just as the deer and antelope in these hills do us."

Tacu was overwhelmed. Recalling his mistrust of Takoda's teachings, he flushed and looked down. "I am honored by this gift, Uncle, and I will keep it with me always." As he closed his fingers around the disk, it rapidly took on the

warmth of his skin. "It amazes me that it comes from so far away, from your own land in the north."

Takoda's eyes gleamed, but otherwise his face showed no emotion. "It could be said that it comes from much farther away than that. The object is called *'nickel.'* I obtained it during my travels." Takoda rose. "Now, Nephew, I want you to go again to the hill tomorrow at dawn. There is more to be learned."

Stricken, Tacu looked across at Takoda. "But Uncle—I thought I had learned what you wished. I thought—I hoped you would allow me to go to the village now."

"Nephew, you have more confidence than I guessed, for apparently you think you have absorbed all the knowledge in *Tovangnar*—the whole world—in two days!" Takoda smiled kindly. "Only the Creator has such ability, and you have just begun to learn, though you are advancing rapidly. Go to your rest now." Takoda acknowledged Rómi with a movement of his head, then walked to the door. He turned again to Tacu. "Each day, decide what you will accomplish and

then let nothing prevent you from doing it." He bent down and left the hut.

Later, Tacu lay on his bed of hides, unable to fall asleep. Again his thoughts whirled, for it seemed the path to his initiation, and to respect from the other young men, and to courtship with a girl from the village, was growing ever longer. He saw the dim shape of his mother, lying on her bed at the other side of the room, and imagined what it would be like if a young maiden lay beside him—his wife. A powerful urge came over him, and he rubbed the soft hides against himself, imagining they were the silky skin of his wife in his arms. The sensation was overwhelmingly pleasurable, but after a few moments he stopped, ashamed, sensing that such action betrayed weakness of will. He would have to earn the right to enjoy such pleasure with his own wife. But he wanted a wife of his own more than anything—more, even, than the approval of the other young men in the village. Finally he slept.

On her side of the hut, Rómi lay facing away from Tacu, eyes open, listening. When her son's

restless motions finally ceased, she closed her eyes and slept too.

FOUR

NEXT MORNING, WHILE STARS STILL SHONE
faintly through a coral haze in the eastern sky, Tacu
stood naked beside the stream that ran by their
hut, holding a soapstone bowl filled with dried
squirrel meat. His exhilaration from the previous

evening had dissipated with his uncle's request to return to the hill, but he felt a lingering wonder at the things his uncle had told him, as well as a new sense of curiosity and anticipation at what the day's instruction might bring. He resolved to see it through. But first, he had an offering to make.

He faced the east and raised the bowl. He spoke silently. "Giver-of-Life, thank you for lending me the strength to overcome my trials yesterday and learn my uncle's lesson. This is my gift to you." He stood with his offering raised for some moments, looking into the magical dawn and considering in what wonder and beauty the spirits must dwell. Then he bent and carefully set the bowl down on the ground. He walked into the cold stream and bathed in preparation for the day.

Once more he lay on the tawny hill, eyes closed but alert to the terrain around him. The cool morning air moving over his body was refreshing, and the peaceful sounds of the awakening grasslands soothed him. The night lingered only in the diminishing croaks of tiny frogs in a creek at

the bottom of the hill. The warming rays of the sun reached him and stretched across the field, pushing the long shadows of the huge oaks before them. He imagined himself as *te-gua,* the sky, looking down upon his territory, yet in touch with the life on the land. As he cast his attention outward, he found his newly won perceptions to be as sharp as they had been yesterday. He felt himself in harmony with the wild land around him and wondered what sense message he would discover today. He felt very light, as though he were the balmy wind, and imagined himself gliding on the breezes, like the red-tailed hawk—higher and higher, the earth spread out below him.

Too late, he heard the rustling of feet moving through the grass and young male voices growing louder. Before he could move, he realized he was caught, and a crawling sense of dread overcame him. The sounds of the footsteps stopped suddenly, a short distance off.

He heard a boy's voice. "What is it?"
Another replied. "It's *na-che*—a man!"
A third voice: "*Pinche*—a body!"

39

Several boys spoke at once.

"He's dead!"

"He was bitten by a rattlesnake!"

Tacu heard more rustling as the intruders came closer. He lay still, with his eyes closed, hating himself for allowing himself to be caught. He wished he were invisible.

"He's not wounded."

"It's one of the People!"

He felt fingers rudely prod his arm and side.

"He's not dead."

He heard some of the footsteps retreat a few feet.

"This man is sick. Maybe we should go tell the *Paha*. Stranger, are you injured?"

Tacu said nothing and remained motionless.

"What are you doing here?"

Tacu didn't respond.

The older boy's voice spoke again. "Wait, I recognize him. It's the *boy* who never came for his initiation!"

"He was afraid to come for initiation?"

"We shouldn't help him. He's a coward."

Embarrassment and rage coursed through Tacu, but he still made no response and kept his eyes shut.

"He's taking a nap in the sun! Nothing else to do, little boy?"

"He's not a boy, he's a woman! Only fit for women's work!"

"Where's your red paint, little girl? You'll get burned sunbathing with no protection!"

Tacu's face flushed, but he didn't move. He didn't understand why they would use such cruel taunts about women and girls; his experience with them was that they were capable and wise, not something debased, as these boys seemed to think. And these boys would all eventually become husbands—did this mean they would treat their future wives and female daughters as beneath contempt?

"She's already getting red in the face. Here, let's cover her up so she doesn't get a bad sunburn!" Tacu felt a stinging pain as a clod of dirt hit him.

More clods followed, thrown harder, accompanied by insults. They hurt, and soon Tacu was covered with dirt, but he still made no response

or movement. To move now would be to show weakness. He willed himself to endure what was happening, take in each detail and taunt, listen to each voice. As he listened, he started to realize that all their bravado was for their own benefit, not his. It was all to save face with each other and each one was competing to seem the most fearless. They didn't actually know anything about *him*; they were just striving to impress each other with ever more outrageous statements. They all sounded like immature boys, even the oldest among them. It came to him that they were no real threat to him; why should he react or respond to their immature and untruthful provocations? While some of them may have gone through the manhood initiation, they were all acting just like children. He would turn this around and teach them a lesson.

"What's wrong with him? Why doesn't he move?"

"Why don't you run into your gopher-hole and suck at your mother's tit, coward?"

Still Tacu did nothing. The young men gathered close around, staring down at him.

42

"He's petrified with fear! He can't move."

"I think he's sick in the head, to lie out here like this. Don't get too close, or you'll get his fever."

The oldest spoke again. "We should go tell the elders about him, so they can banish him. He's not right in his head."

In that instant, Tacu's eyes popped open and the boys jumped back. He saw seven young men ranging in age from six to seventeen, and he knew he could best any of them. He glared at them without twitching a muscle or speaking, projecting himself to be as fierce as *piwil*, his great-grandfather the grizzly. All at once he uttered a roar and sprang upward into a fighting crouch, his knife in his hand. The boys shrieked in terror and fled in all directions.

Tacu looked after them, watching their dust resettle. He had never created such an effect on anyone, and he began to laugh. As he laughed, he found he was laughing not just at the boys, but also at himself and all his needless months of fear and worry over what the young men at the village thought of him. He laughed for many moments, and

when he stopped, he felt as light as the downy seeds that floated from the trees in the season of new growth.

He looked down at himself, saw that he was still covered in dust and dirt, and realized that his appearance must have made him even more frightening as he sprang up. The boys had unwittingly made him more formidable to themselves and never realized it. He laughed again, then brushed himself off and set out for home.

FIVE

THE SUN IS RIGHT BEFORE HIM AS HE IS THRUST
into the air—he reaches out, delighted, to grasp it, a
golden ball. But a dark shadow, racing him for it, takes it
in his mouth and swallows it whole, and its golden light
shines out of a brilliant eye. Soft feathers brush by him,

ruffling his hair with their wind, and he laughs. Then he is falling, and he catches a last glimpse of his father, banking on the wind and rising back to the spirits. He laughs again and reaches his arms toward the sky.

Tacu came awake suddenly. His mother stood before his bed in the transparent, mysterious blue light of the early dawn, looking down at him. He felt this must be a vision, a waking dream, for she was dressed as he had never seen her, in beaded and feathered leggings and white tunic, with a bonnet decorated with shells and many white eagle feathers. Her face was painted red. When she did not disappear, he realized, with shock, that he was indeed awake. He sat up and waited for her to speak. Her expression was stern, but he could see love in her eyes.

"Son, I travel this morning *páymi*—west—to fast and make vigil at *Asawtngna,* the Place of the Eagle. It is long past the time I should do this, for I am *Panes*, White-headed Eagle Maiden. I go to pray to the Giver-of-Life for a vision." She looked solemn. "I will be gone for two or three days."

"What is wrong, Mother? Has something happened?"

"No, but a change approaches for which I must seek guidance."

"May I not travel with you, to help and protect you, Mother? It is a difficult climb."

"No, no creature will harm *Panes*. It is my duty to go alone to seek the help of my spirit-guide." She smiled at him, relieving his worry. "I am very proud of you, my son. You progress rapidly and are learning things far beyond your years. While I am away, go and find a new place where we can gather plants and herbs. Go into the hills, in the direction of *Topangna,* and search those canyons." She gave him an appraising look. "Perhaps you will also find opportunities to test yourself and your new skills." Rómi bent to embrace him, then stood, turned and left the hut.

Tacu sat motionless, overwhelmed. His own mother was *Panes*, the most holy woman in the village, one who had been reborn as a deity after her vision quest! Then he turned pale, all at once recalling many times when he had been short with

47

her, disrespectful or angry. To show disrespect to a holy elder was sacrilege, an offense punishable by banishment from the village. He felt very ashamed. Then unbidden thoughts entered his mind, making him think that perhaps the rules didn't apply to his family and he was safe from banishment, since he and his mother lived outside the village and did not participate in the community's ceremonies.

He thought again of his mother, standing in the early light, dressed all in white, and he felt shame at even having considered finding a way to exempt himself from the rules or avoid his just punishment. He decided he must do all he could to make amends to her for his past transgressions and his present cowardice. The only thing he could think of right now was to go and find as many herbs as possible, as she had requested. And he would kill small game and dry the meat to replenish the stores in their *kich*.

Tacu got up and went outside to bathe in the stream. Back inside, he dressed, then took some parched wild oat meal from a covered container and made it his breakfast. After he had cleaned his bowl, he hung his stone hunting knife, sling, and a

small bundle of sinew twine from his belt. Then he opened a covered pot and carefully removed a strip of pemmican, made from dried meat, fat, and *kochar*—dried currants and gooseberries—and put it into a small deerskin pouch on his belt. He also tied a large milkweed fiber net bag to his belt to hold the plants he found. He gathered up his small-game bow, some wood-tipped arrows, and his curved throwing stick and stepped through the doorway. Outside, he loosened one end of a tule mat tied above the *kich* door so it fell down to cover the entrance. Then he turned and started toward the mountains that lay to the south.

As the cool morning passed into balmy midday, Tacu walked into unfamiliar territory. He pushed through dense, pungent thickets of manzanita and scrub oak, whose sharp branches scratched and pulled at him. He scrambled over ridges rough with rose and white rock outcroppings, and descended through narrow, rocky canyons. Some of these carried creeks that were no greater than a trickle. In one white-rock bluff he found a thick, oily black substance oozing

from the rock. He put his finger in it, then tasted it. It tasted foul and he immediately spit it out. This must be the tar that people in the village used to seal water baskets and fasten arrowheads to their shafts.

Now and then he found a likely plant for his mother, broke off several of its branches and carefully placed them in his net pouch. Though he startled several *toovit*—brush rabbits—and other small rodents, he let them go, planning to hunt after he had gathered enough plants. So he kept on, looking for an area in which he could harvest many plants. He was delighted with each new vista, and felt adventurous and strong.

Ascending a large canyon, Tacu scrambled up the steep stream bed, climbing over the scattered boulders and crossing the small rivulet of water that had created its own smaller canyon within the large one. Occasionally he came upon large trees with mottled white, tan and gray trunks and huge light green leaves. Some of them grew from the ground leaning sideways, so that he could walk right up the trunk.

51

He became aware of a rushing sound in
the distance—fast-running water. Soon he found
himself among clumps of tall trees with sharp, dark
green quills in place of leaves. Coming around a
bend, the miniature stream he had been following
dead-ended in a near-vertical rock wall about five
times his height. The rushing sound was much
louder, and many small ribbons of water dropped
down the face, making the rocks shine. Tacu had
to scale the cliff if he wanted to move ahead, but it
did not present an obstacle to him because he had
climbed the rocky bluffs and cliffs at the Place of
the Stones many times.

He agilely picked his way from ledge to ledge
over the wet rocks until he reached the top. As
he stepped up over the edge of the face, he found
himself on a stony saddle between two higher peaks.
The rushing sound was a deafening roar. He crossed
to the other side, looked down and gasped. Below
him, a tremendous frothing blue-white torrent of
water gushed into the air out of a large gap in the
stone wall and fell, flanked by a wide wreath of
mist, down the stone face to disappear into a thick

growth of dark green trees below. He had never seen such water and found it awe-inspiring. This was a place of power, and he looked about, expecting a spirit to appear on the path beside him. He offered a silent prayer of thanks to the Giver-of-Life, then crouched on the edge and remained there motionless for many minutes, gazing at the roaring waterfall below him.

Finally he decided to move onward. As he looked out over the woods below, he saw a bit of brighter green at a distance. It could be a meadow, nourished by the water flowing down from the fall. He walked along the ridge until he found a likely route down the cliff, then descended rapidly, leaping from ledge to ledge like the large cats that hunted the canyons.

At the bottom, he found himself in a cool dense growth of the dark quill-trees. The forest floor was cushioned with rust-red quills that had fallen from the trees, and the air was pungent with their sharp aroma. They were not unlike porcupine quills. He scooped up several handfuls to bring back to his mother. He heard the soft "whoo-whoo" of his little brother, the owl,

from the branches above and was glad of the familiar greeting as he passed.

Soon the light grew brighter, signaling fresher, more varied vegetation ahead. He walked up a gradual rise. He could hear the rushing of the cliff-waters off to his right through the trees. As he topped the rise, he looked down into a lush wonderland—a large, rolling patchwork of green meadows and small groves of sapling woods that were criss-crossed and nourished by small streams that fed into the larger one. Birds sang from the young trees and white, yellow and blue butterflies floated from plant to plant. This rich meadow seemed like it had been dropped from the heavens, carpeted as it was by hundreds of different plants and colorful flowers. He had never seen such bounty.

Tacu looked around carefully to make sure he was alone, then descended into the meadow and began slowly picking his way through. He could see that the meadow was a rich source of both food and medicinal plants. He was also happy to see a profusion of *soar*—rushes—lining the banks of the

stream. They could be gathered later for weaving baskets and making mats to leach the acorn meal. He easily spotted the yellow flowers of *takape ahots*—bladder pod. When he saw the flat, elongated, bluish-lavender leaves of *kasili*—white sage—one of the most versatile and important herbs, he said a prayer of thanks to the Creator for leading him to this plant, which his people called "grandmothers." His mother would have many uses for it, and his uncle might also wish to smoke its dried leaves in the evening, when he came to their house. Tacu carefully harvested samples of the plants as he moved, tucking them into his net pouch. His mother would be very happy. And today the meadow should also yield as many brush rabbits and ground squirrels as he wished to carry, if his aim was sharp. He inhaled the rich, scented air and felt a deep satisfaction.

At the far end of the meadow, before the land rose again, stood the largest oak he had ever seen. Its branches formed a gigantic tangled sphere that reached upward to many times a man's height. He had an idea: if he hid himself on a low branch

55

among the abundant leaves, he could spot small game from above and pick it off with an arrow or his sling. While this was not the usual way to hunt, he wanted to try it. He moved toward the tree, selecting and picking herbs as he went.

By the time he was a few yards from the tree, he had gathered a bursting selection of desirable plants. He made sure they were tucked securely into his pouch, then walked under the oak's canopy. The tree's outermost branches drooped almost to the ground, creating a cool, shaded enclosure that shielded him from outside view. He imagined that it was just like entering a huge *Yobangnar*—the large community hut in which the most sacred religious rituals and ceremonies were celebrated. Many of the precious acorns had fallen under the tree and still lay about. Tacu wondered why they had not been gathered so that the *chemeshkwar*—acorn meat—could be leached and made into acorn meal. Perhaps it was that this meadow lay so far from any village.

He had just surveyed the space enclosed by the tree's branches, and tilted his head to look for a

likely branch from which to hunt, when a piercing war cry rang out. He whirled and his field of vision was split by the stark image of a warrior in full war regalia and paint in mid-leap above him, stone knife aimed for his heart. Tacu froze, recovered, then lurched to the right, falling just as the knife came down. It grazed his left arm and whicked into the earth beside him. In the next instant Tacu was on his feet, his own knife in hand. He cast himself onto the warrior—but he was no longer there. Tacu threw himself into a roll to regain sight of the brave, but as he came onto his back, the sinewy form flew onto him and Tacu saw the warrior's face above him, an inch from his own, cheeks drawn back in a killing grimace. Tacu felt the point of the blade depressing the soft skin between his ribs. Fury swept through him and in spite of the blade at his heart, he pushed the brave's body away. In the same movement, with a deep-throated howl, he thrust his own knife hard up, intending to slit the man's throat. Instead, his blade glanced off the warrior's jaw and raked across his face. Half of the face peeled away to reveal a bloody grinning skull whose open jaw fell onto his neck. At the same instant, he felt a cascade of intense, arcing pain in his chest and knew he had been impaled. Everything went black.

SIX

THE WORLD WAS RED, AND THERE MUST BE

nothing left of him but blood. It was the death that every warrior hoped for. Except that if he were dying, there should be pain. But there was no pain, and somehow this spoiled his dying.

He thrust himself toward consciousness, anxious to find the pain and fulfill his warrior's destiny. As he did this, the redness localized over his eyes—but he still felt no pain. Annoyed, he swam the final distance to consciousness and opened his eyes. Above him he saw hints of blue sky through oak leaves and the partially obscured orb of the sun. He lay for ten heartbeats, trying to take it in, then put his hand up to feel his chest. It was whole and sound. How could it be?

He jerked to a sitting position and looked all around him. There was no warrior's body and no blood. Unperturbed birdsong filled the air. Where was the evidence of his mortal struggle? How could he still be alive? He got to his feet and stood looking around, very disturbed. His knife lay a few feet away. He picked it up and examined it—it was clean, bearing no trace of the warrior's blood. He wiped his hand across the back of his left arm, where the warrior's blade had initially grazed him. He felt moisture, and when he looked at his hand, it contained a small smear of blood. Disbelieving, he wiped his arm again, and again there was

blood—this was the arm the warrior's blade had cut. Thoroughly confused, Tacu turned around, surveying the ground for footsteps or other sign of the warrior, then circled the tree trunk, doing the same. There was no sign, though the leaves and dirt under the tree were disturbed where he had been lying.

He crouched and peered under the edge of the oak's canopy in all directions. He could see no one. Baffled, he sighed. He had no way to solve this puzzle, but it was yet daylight and he still must kill some game before he returned to his home. He stood.

Still wary, he quickly set about stringing his bow with a fiber bowstring, glancing around frequently. He would use his bow rather than throwing stick, in case the warrior returned. Once the bow was ready, he took a big breath, walked to the edge of the canopy, then looked up into the branches to find a seat.

Immediately he locked gazes with a pair of large brown eyes, and nearly dropped his bow in surprise. A girl was perched on a branch just above

his head, her eyes fixed on him. She appeared to be somewhere near Tacu's age. Her black hair was long and thick and fell down over shapely shoulders to her waist. From her neck hung several strands of tiny shell beads and a garland of wildflowers. She had a small tattoo on her chin, and her cheeks and chest were reddened with ochre. She wore a long grass skirt.

Tacu didn't know what to say for a moment. "Maiden, why are you here by yourself in this tree?"

The girl looked away shyly, but then looked back and indicated her own reed basket balanced in a crook of the branch. Like his pouch, it, too, was filled with plants and herbs.

Tacu looked at her quizzically. "That doesn't explain why you sit in the tree."

The girl finally spoke. "I was gathering herbs over there—" She gestured to the side of the tree opposite that from which Tacu had come. "—when I heard you approach. I thought you might be a bear, or a *Topangnavit*—villager from Topanga—so I went up into the tree." She looked at him critically. "But you are neither." The girl picked up her basket and began

63

to climb down agilely. When she reached the ground, she started walking away quickly.

"Wait! Stay and talk with me!" The girl fascinated Tacu.

The girl turned, hesitating. "I am not permitted to speak to strangers."

"I am not a stranger—I am Tacu!"

She giggled. "So Tacu is never a stranger. Well then, answer me this: why did you roll around in the leaves under the tree, grunting and crying?"

Tacu blushed furiously. "I—I was trying to rid myself of fleas from the meadow!"

"With your knife?"

Tacu blushed again. "I—well—" He straightened. "Yes, that's how I do it."

She laughed at his embarrassment. "No matter. I could see that you were practicing to fight, and believe me, you were so fierce that I was very frightened."

Again Tacu was speechless, but this time with pleasure.

The girl looked down, shy again. "Any girl would like a husband who is as fierce as you to protect her."

Tacu's heart began to pound, and he gathered his courage. "Will you marry me?" He immediately saw his mistake. "Uh, I mean, are you already betrothed?"

The girl covered her mouth with her hand, smiling. "No, I am not betrothed."

"May I court you?"

"What village are you from?"

Tacu hesitated. "I live with my mother in the west hills. Our village is near the Place of the Stones."

The girl looked him up and down. His upper right arm did not bear the small brand that signified initiation into manhood. She frowned. "You have not been initiated. Yet you want to marry me?"

He just looked at her, embarrassed, trying to think of what to say.

"Though you don't look so young, I cannot marry an uninitiated man. I would be shamed and my parents would never allow it. *Yami uimi*—I am going."

She turned, but Tacu moved forward and touched her arm gently. "I am learning from my

65

uncle—a wise elder. Once I become initiated, which will be very soon, will you favor me?"

She looked him over for a moment. "You are very handsome, though strange looking. I have never seen a man who looks like you." Then she smiled hesitantly. "If you fulfill your vision quest and are initiated, and my parents approve, you may court me. Don't come before then. When you come to my parents' *kich*, you must announce yourself outside. Bring my father a gift of many beads, and for me a soft hide cloth and a basket. I am Wesara." She turned again and walked away.

Tacu unconsciously fingered his long, copper-tinged braid and watched the girl until she disappeared into the trees and shrubs. His heart was still pounding, but to his anxiety had been added hope. With the prospect of being able to court her after his initiation and vision quest, he knew that this was what he wanted more than anything. He would build a new home for them near his parent's hut, and they would cultivate the edible plants that his mother said would grow there. If only his uncle would allow him go to the village for his initiation

now! Surely he had learned enough to be allowed to go. He would ask Takoda again.

He thought again of his fight with the mysterious warrior. He wanted to know what his uncle would say about it. Tacu decided to carry out his hunt in the usual way, on foot, to save time. With his bow and sling at the ready, he walked back into the meadow.

SEVEN

WHEN TACU RETURNED HOME AFTER DARK,
the hut was empty. Though Tacu knew his mother
would keep her vigil for several days, he was unused
to her absence. In her calm way, she was always
in complete control of the household. After a few

moments, he realized he would have to prepare food for his uncle in her place, so he got the fire going and set about skinning and preparing one of the hares he had caught. He would roast hare for Takoda and have acorn meal himself—it was unlucky to eat the game you had killed yourself.

In a little while, a shadow appeared in the doorway and Takoda entered.

"*Nachochan,* Nephew."

"*Miyuu*—welcome. Sit down and eat."

Takoda seated himself by the fire and took the bowl of roasted rabbit that Tacu offered him. After taking a few bites, he looked up at Tacu. "You have done well to bring such flavorful food back from your hunt." He leisurely ate the rest of his meal, then set his bowl down and took up his pipe. He carefully filled the pipe with tobacco, then lit it. After taking a long pull of smoke, from which he obviously derived great pleasure, he turned his attention to Tacu and observed him closely.

"Once again you have had an eventful day. Yesterday you had an encounter with boys from the village, and today—?"

"Yes, Uncle." Tacu was surprised that Takoda knew about his adventure with the boys. Takoda waited.

"Uncle, today something happened which I don't understand. In the meadow where I was gathering plants for our stores, I was attacked by a warrior from a tribe I did not recognize. We fought fiercely, and then I killed him at the same time I felt myself wounded to the death by his blade—even though my presence now contradicts this story. All became dark, for how long I do not know. Then I awoke, alive and uninjured but for a small cut on my arm—and there was no sign of the warrior. Yet I had felt his bloody carcass fall upon me as we each wounded the other to the death!"

"How did the struggle begin?"

"The warrior leapt upon me from the branch of an oak tree. I escaped his initial attack, except for a light stroke from his knife—then he fell on me again and as I slashed his face, I felt him thrust his blade into my chest—" Tacu ran his hands over his unblemished upper torso once again.

"Show me the wound on your arm."

Tacu showed Takoda the cut, now covered by a line of dried blood.

"Were you resting when the warrior attacked you?"

"No, Uncle—I had just walked under the oak, from which I planned to hunt game. I had had no time to fall asleep."

Takoda sat silent, considering.

"And what was the nature of this warrior?"

"Uncle, he was as solid as my own flesh. I felt his weight upon me, and I felt the pain as I succumbed."

"Nephew, the spirits have tested you with a vision. You must contemplate this experience and decide its meaning for yourself."

"But Uncle, I have not fasted nor partaken of *manit*—jimson root drink—in the initiation ceremony. How could I have a vision?"

Takoda waited a moment, then spoke. "Listen to me now. When the spirits have something to say, they do not wait for permission. They do not wait until we have gone to the village, danced and drunk, if there is something

important to say! Think about it: would this make sense? Therefore, your own sight, smell, touch, must be your first and last resort, even if things happen to you that you cannot explain. Trust your experience."

Tacu hesitated. "Uncle, why would the spirit choose me, when I have not yet studied and worshiped with the *Paha?*"

"This world is transparent and many spirits walk here with us. Some of the people see things as they really are, and in their knowing way, the spirits know when someone is ready. You fought bravely and survived the spirit warrior's ambush. Others have not survived. Few men are granted a trial directly by the spirits. You were chosen, and you have proved yourself worthy. So it is."

Tacu blushed furiously and looked down. "I am honored, Uncle. But what does it mean?"

Takoda looked at him with an amused glint in his eye. "Your accomplishment shows what it shows. If I say any more, you will become insufferable and fit only for the company of *jungnaá*—the buzzard." Takoda's face grew serious.

"Perhaps you will prevail in life and become respected and wise."

Tacu began to demur modestly but Takoda interrupted. "No, do not deny this. Never make less of your strength or ability. Fear not to state anything, if it is true." He drew from his pipe again. "I have said it before: if you remain true to yourself, your family, your community and the Creator, you will retain your abilities, and your strength will only increase." Takoda set his pipe down next to his food bowl. He stood.

"Tomorrow I will instruct you further, and we will truly see how far your learning has progressed. Prepare for a journey."

"Yes, Uncle." Tacu thought of the beautiful girl he had met in the meadow. "Uncle, there is something else I wish to know—?"

"That is very good! Tomorrow you shall know it." Takoda smiled and got up.

"But—"

"*Yamu uimi*—I am going."

Tacu sighed. "*Mea.*"

After Takoda had left, Tacu took a few quick mouthfuls of acorn meal, then set down his bowl

and noticed that Takoda had left his pipe. He ran
to the doorway and called "Uncle!" But Takoda
was gone. Tacu re-entered and reverently picked
up Takoda's pipe from where he had left it beside
his place at the fire. A red glow in the pipe bowl
showed that the sacred tobacco was still lit. Tacu
was baffled, for Takoda was usually meticulous in
the care of his pipe. He lifted the pipe by its stem
to look at it closely, and as he did so, a gust of
night wind blew through the doorway, making the
fire waver and spit. An instant later, a small tendril
of smoke rose from the pipe and took the form of
the red-tailed hawk. As it drifted away from him, it
stretched its wings high, powerfully stroked them
down, then disappeared. When he looked into the
pipe, it had gone out.

Tacu realized he had truly walked with
the spirits that day, and thoughtfully went about
clearing the implements of their meal. After
emptying the tobacco ashes into the fire, he
respectfully placed the pipe on a separate mat for
Takoda. He wiped out the food bowl and put it
away. Then he lay down on his bed and had only

a moment to realize how truly exhausted he was before he was asleep.

He stood, dwarfed and alone in a huge village made of immense gleaming crystal and shiny black obsidian spires. The flat ground beneath his feet was made of tiny stones, crushed and sealed with the thick black tar that seeped from the rocks in the hills. He knew he was not far from his village near the Place of the Stones, and began to walk. But he was lost, and could see no way out of the strange village. He heard the wind rushing and tilted back his head. Far above him, over the tops of the spires, an eagle soared, going in and out of sight. Tacu walked, following the eagle. It landed at the very top of an obsidian dwelling that reflected the other dwellings in its glossy sides. He drew near, and its side opened. His mother came out, wearing her White Eagle Maiden regalia. She looked at Tacu with great love, and said, "Our people flourish and multiply once more in this, our homeland." She looked back inside the dwelling. A tall man in a shining white tunic and leggings of the same material came to the opening and stood looking at him. From the quality of his spirit, he knew it was Takoda,

*although his features were different. Takoda nodded
to him, and Tacu moved forward. But as he neared the
opening, a chestnut-skinned young man with the long
black hair of the* Tongva *moved up beside Takoda. Tacu
saw that he should remain outside, for the young man was
himself, and Tacu realized that he dwelt and studied here
with Takoda. The young man looked at Tacu, then said to
him, indicating Takoda, "He has returned to us. His name
in the tongue of his forebears in the North, and in the
tongue of this age also, means 'friend to everyone.'" Takoda
smiled at Tacu, and a great sense of peace washed through
him.*

EIGHT

WHEN TACU AWOKE, IT WAS STILL DARK.
Takoda had returned. Unlike most days, his long
black hair was rolled into a topknot. To this he had
attached a simple ornament decorated with quills
and three large eagle tail feathers, standing erect

in the manner of his people, the *Siksika*. He was rebuilding the fire and had taken out some of the brush rabbit Tacu had prepared the night before. Tacu got up and went to sit beside him as he ate.

"Good morning, Uncle."

Takoda acknowledged him, then picked up a plantain-leaf wrapped package from beside him. "Here is meat I killed for you."

"Thank you, Uncle." Tacu took the bundle and placed it carefully to the side. He looked up at Takoda, hopeful.

"Uncle, there is a maiden I wish to court."

Takoda gave him his attention.

"She was in the oak tree after my vision yesterday. I must go soon to the village to seek out the *Paha* and proceed with my initiation, because if I do not, this maiden will not speak to me."

"Ah, you have met a tree spirit, hey?" Takoda chuckled. "Make sure that she is not just another vision from that tree!"

Tacu looked worried, and Takoda laughed. "Nephew—I am certain that she is actual, and I am pleased that you wish to marry. I ask that you

wait until my instruction is complete. With this preparation, you will understand your initiation far better."

Tacu's hopeful expression faded. He sighed and looked down. "But Uncle, I fear that she will marry another if I do not begin courting her soon. She will not speak to me again until I have undergone the initiation ceremonies."

"Do not trouble yourself—the time will not be long." Takoda put down his food bowl. "Nephew, I will not be with you much longer."

Tacu was shocked. "Uncle—I did not expect this. I thought you would be with us always."

"I will stay only a short while longer. You are in truth now capable of caring and providing for your mother, and a wife and children. I must go to prepare the way for you to follow me, in your own time."

"I will be following you...later?"

Takoda smiled kindly. "Much later. You will soon understand."

"Does my mother know you will be leaving us?"

"There is little that your mother does not know. Even so, she seeks the guidance of her spirit helper."

Tacu was silent for a moment. "Uncle, my mother has revealed to me that she is *Panes*."

"Your mother is a holy and wise spirit."

"I am ashamed at my treatment of her." Tacu looked down in shame. "I have too often dishonored her—spoken sharply to her, in impatience, or disregarded her counsel. If I had only known—"

"—you would have treated her better?"

Tacu nodded.

"It is good that you have realized this and told me. It takes character to admit a misdeed."

Tacu looked relieved.

Takoda went on. "Now, tell me, does not *any* woman, any member of your family or your village— or any honorable member of the People—deserve such respect?"

"But the *tsinitsnits*—wise man—or *Panes*—are they not worthy of more reverence?..." Tacu's voice faded as it came to him what Takoda meant. "Uncle, I am even more shamed. I have had thought only of

myself. Knowing this, I do not feel that I deserve the respect of the villagers now. Is there anything I may do to make amends?"

"You will have many opportunities, as time passes, to do good for your family and your village. See that you do so. For now, remember and heed what you have just realized, for this is one of the most important things a man must know—to respect each person, to face your misdeeds honestly, and then to learn, so as not to repeat them." Takoda smiled kindly. "Now, what else was it you wished to ask me?"

Tacu looked at Takoda in surprise. He seemed to know what was in Tacu's mind even before Tacu knew it.

"My mother has said little to me about my father. I would like to know more about him."

"His story is entwined with that of your mother. This much you may know. When your mother was young, she was chosen from among many girls to become *Panes*. She went to the mountains during the Eagle feast and had a powerful vision, as the village elders foretold. The

legends of your people say that during the vigil of
this maiden, she dies and is reborn as White-headed
Eagle Maiden. During her vision, your mother saw
far into the future. Your mother was transformed.
She wished to tell your people what she had learned,
but they did not understand what she told them
and disregarded it. She wished to help her people as
shaman, but the village chief at that time forbade it
because he felt her teachings would sow too much
confusion. But the true reason was that he did not
understand what she said either. Though her own
family and many in the village honored her, her
purpose was thwarted."

Tacu leaned forward, stricken at hearing of
his mother's long-ago dilemma, so like the one he
felt presently. "What did my mother do?"

"She spent much time alone, in
contemplation. During one such vigil, she came
upon a man with skin as white as the chalk in the
hills—hungry, lost and in need. He spoke a strange
tongue, but they were able to speak through signs.
Your mother did not hesitate, but helped him—for
the tradition of your people is to be kind to others,

even though they know them not. She brought him food and tended him until he was well. During his recovery, they gradually came to be able to understand one another. His name was Agustin. He was from a land across two great oceans. His people were fighting men and came to our world to take control of the earth. They also planned to force your people to forsake their own traditions and adopt their own, and make them work for them and adhere to their foreign ways. But your father was unlike them: he did not want to do this, so he left his people.

Tacu mouthed the name, which felt strange on his tongue. "A-gus-tin."

"After he was well, he asked your mother to join with him as his wife, and she accepted. They settled here, on this rich land apart from the village, and you were born. Your father showed your mother how to grow the edible plants of his own people. As I was traveling in this land, I came to your parents' *kich*. We came to know each other, and your parents became as my brother and sister. After your father left this life, I took upon myself your

86

teaching. You are the offspring of two great streams, the nations of your father and your mother. Your course is therefore different from that of any other youth in your village. I am here to guide you to the knowledge you will need to live and thrive."

Tacu felt conflicting emotions. "Uncle, I never knew my father or his story. And I must truly make amends to my mother, for she is one for whose sacred power might never be noticed, since she lives a simple life and does not speak of it."

"You will have many opportunities in the days to come. Do not let it sit too heavily in your heart. Eat quickly and get ready, so that we may start. We are going into the mountains."

NINE

TAKODA AND TACU CLIMBED THROUGH STEEP,
thickly wooded canyons and up over red sandstone
ridges made of many angled layers piled above each
other. Finally, they stood at the top of a narrow
ridge, so high they could see a great distance

in all directions. Their vantage point seemed to span three worlds. On one side, to the west, Tacu could see range after range of mountains fading into smoky blue mist for an immense distance. If he turned to the northeast, in the direction from which they had come, Tacu could see, far below, the western edge of the great valley where *Tototngna* lay. And with a final turn to his right he could see, so far below them that it looked like it was in another world, a long, curved white strip sparkling along the eastern edge of a great expanse of deep blue. The blue reached far into the distance and rose all the way up to the line where sight stopped, so that it appeared as high as the mountain on which they stood. This was Tacu's first view of the ocean, even though it was from a great distance.

The immense sweep of land and sea took away his breath. He felt that he could see the whole world—*Tovangnar*. Exhilarated, he turned to Takoda expectantly.

Takoda pointed. "Far below us there, out of sight, is the village of *Topangna*, near the ocean. Farther south are the territories of many people

who are all your distant kin, all *Tongva*. This is
a holy place." Without preamble, he stepped to
the edge of the saddle and looked out over the
mountains and canyons dropping down to the sea in
the distance. "This is my song." With his arms raised
partway, he began a haunting, wavering chant.

> Oh great spirits of these mountains,
> we see you and give our thanks!
> Help us to gain the wisdom
> to live a life of honor and respect
> for the gifts that you share with us.
>
> We come to renew ourselves,
> to stand on your weathered shoulder,
> to reach down to the roots of your massive trunk
> and from your granite sinews and wooded flesh,
> partake of your strength and know it as our own.
>
> I hear you say many things to me
> with the insistent wind, your breath.
> Your wise words rush against my ears,
> and bring to ecstasy my leaping soul.
> Earthly embodiment of the great spirits,

you share with me an ancient vision
as my grandfather, as my kin.

This song is for you, our ancestors,
ghost mountains of the time before time.
Your faint outlines range back into memory
like your rolling cousins beyond this ridge,
fading, fold upon fold, into the flowing mist.

Into my heart you speak in the tongues of
rushing streams, uttering your tales in words
formed in the murmuring, fleeing flood,
where the rolling river stones speak
a million words that still make thunder fall.

Many ages have passed since your first song,
a roar in molten flame, rolling across the land,
when the sculpting hand of the Creator
cast his own likeness into massive stones,
and you first came to be.
I hear you now, as in wildfire, in spring rain,
in leaf-broken breeze you speak to me, and say:
"We are the oldest ones, so heavy in our

tortured, flame-molded creation,
heavy beyond all tears—
But hear us: we are still no more than ghosts
wavering before you, Children of the Earth.

"In form you seem like fragile children
balanced on our craggy knees,
But you too are makers of worlds
and all the vast drifting spaces—
You are Spirit, like us, and made of the
living force that binds us all into shape."

Takoda raised his arms to the sky, then
continued.

Oh, spirit of our Father Sun
and our Mother Earth,
hear my prayer,
Grant us the wisdom to know and to act
In keeping with your great Plan.

Takoda looked into the distance for a few
moments, and it seemed to Tacu that he was also

93

looking into a different time and place. Then he turned to Tacu.

"Now, Nephew, I want you, once more, to lie on the earth with your eyes closed, while I pray." Takoda gestured to Tacu to lie in front of him, then lifted his head and closed his eyes.

Tacu lay on his back, gazing into the deep blue above him for a moment. Then he closed his own eyes.

He floated high on a warm updraft, his wings spread wide to take advantage of every change in the air, the orange-red feathers in his tail spread for stability and lift. He surveyed the ground far below. A movement in the grass. A pocket mouse exited its burrow cautiously and scurried a short distance away, then stopped and sniffed the air.

He lowered his head, pulled in his wings and dove. The ground rushed up toward him as though he was hail falling from the sky, and he knew he would die.

"No! No!" Tacu's arms flailed as he tried to push the rushing earth away from him. "No!" His eyes

94

flew open. He blinked, looked around, and realized where he was.

Takoda sat near him, observing.

Tacu flushed. "Uncle, I flew as a hawk and—and was falling from the sky."

"Nephew, set your mind to face whatever vision comes. Close your eyes."

Nothing stirred below him, and he flew on. He adjusted the tips of his wings and began rising in a wide, oblique spiral. After eight revolutions, he leveled off and drifted across the ridge, eyes sweeping the rocky terrain below. A brown brush rabbit twitched its ears from where it sat, and without thought, Tacu dropped toward it, a living arrow. The earth and the animal exploded in size as they bulged toward him and then he had the desperately wriggling rabbit in his unforgiving talons. He rose again into the sky, squeezing and crushing until, in a brief moment, the rabbit's movements ceased and he knew without thought that he would eat and live.

Tacu opened his eyes and looked at Takoda, dazed. He felt very strange and large, as though

he were the entire volume of air sitting above the land. "Uncle, I had a vision that I was a hawk, and I killed a rabbit. But this troubles me: how am I to understand this vision...?"

Takoda did not reply, but gestured for him to close his eyes once more.

He felt good, in a way that did not include thought. His children suckled at their mother's teats and he had found many tender leaves to push into the nest with her. He pushed them closer, within reach of his mate. The earth inside their tunnel was warm, and his offspring would grow large rapidly. He crawled up toward the circle of light at the top of his tunnel. He would find more leaves for his family. He put his face into the opening and sniffed. Nothing. He crawled up so that his body was halfway out, twitching his head around and still smelling the air: only the usual scents of earth and chaparral. He came all the way out of his tunnel, looked around, then jumped across the ground toward a likely bush. He heard a soft "whoosh" and looked up. Too late!—a feathered whirlwind smelling like death fell on him. There was an explosion of intense pain in his torso, and for a brief moment he saw the

earth start to drop away below him; then there was blackness.

Tacu felt a tremor—his body was shaking through some force outside himself, and someone was calling his name. But he couldn't move. His body hurt in every fiber.

"Nephew, rouse yourself. Open your eyes."

The voice grew louder, and he knew he should obey. He tried to open his eyes, but they were crushed pulp, and he couldn't.

"Tacu. Open your eyes. Take hold of your body."

Somehow, that made sense, so he did. His eyes flicked open, and he saw Takoda leaning above him. The pain receded. He was lying on his back. He pushed himself up and Takoda helped him. He remembered what had happened and felt confused and angry.

"Uncle, I was a rabbit—the same rabbit who fell prey to the red-tailed hawk. I was crushed, then eaten. I suffered the pain of its death. I was helpless, I would never see my mate again—" Tacu

let out an involuntary sob. "Why must I feel what the rabbit felt? I was helpless—I could do nothing to save myself. I do not know what to think of this. What kind of lesson can this be; it does not seem right."

Takoda's eyes glinted. "Lie again. There is more."

Reluctantly, Tacu lay back down on the dirt and closed his eyes.

He felt an explosion of intense pain, then blackness and nothing. All at once it was bright again, and he saw the earth spreading rapidly out beneath him, wider and wider as he rose. He was alone, and felt no pain. Then his field of vision encompassed a hawk carrying something in its talons—the torn remains of a small gray-brown rabbit. Distantly, he knew that that had been himself, his body, though he felt quite separate from it now. He felt light and good, and the field of his sight grew so that he saw the entire lush landscape below him in all directions at once. Far, far beneath him on a small ridge in the mountains were two tiny human forms, one black-haired, standing, looking up into the air at him, and the other lying flat with

its copper hair spread around it and its eyes closed. Then his attention shifted, and he was in a dark, cool rabbit warren. A mother rabbit in her nest was giving birth, and he recognized her from her scent—it was his mother. He squirmed beneath her in the warm darkness, his tiny eyes still closed, searching, reaching up for the nourishment that would allow him to live.

Tacu's eyes opened, and he sat up and looked at Takoda in wonder. He didn't know what to say.

Takoda turned and walked a few steps away, his back to Tacu. "Nephew, you wanted to know, 'What am I? Am I the hawk? Am I a rabbit?' So now, I ask you to consider carefully. What are you?"

Tacu stared at Takoda's back as he tried to understand his experience.

"I am one of the People, a boy. Soon to be a man."

"That is right. And what more?"

Tacu faltered, then grimaced, impatient. "This makes no sense to me. What does it matter if I have a vision that I am a rabbit, or a hawk? That is not what I am."

99

Takoda turned back to him. His face revealed no emotion. "For now, accept that your visions have a meaning which you are to discover. Did not the circumstances of your visions appear and feel real?"

"Yes, Uncle, they did. That is what troubles me."

"All right. Consider them as you might any memory. Incorporate them into your experience and use them when considering how you reply to my questions."

Tacu frowned.

"I will seek to do so, Uncle, but I—I fear to look back at these experiences."

"Remember your courage in fighting the spirit warrior, and your willingness to die a warrior's death." Takoda sat down on the ground near Tacu. "Let us proceed, then. Consider further: what are you?"

"Uncle, this seems very obvious, anyone could know this. I am Tacu."

Takoda nodded. "Yes, you are right. And what more?"

Tacu recalled his vision, striving to understand it. "I was the hawk, then the newborn rabbit.

"Good. And what else are you?"

"I am—the son of my mother, Rómi, and my father."

"Indeed. And what more?"

"I am—of my father's blood, a traveler?"

"Yes. And what more?"

"There is no more. That is all." Tacu stretched. "Uncle, may I rise?"

Takoda got up. "Let us walk a short way."

Tacu got to his feet and looked around him. "Truly this is the most beautiful place I have seen, Uncle." Below them to the south, down the slope, was a huge flat abutment of red sandstone rising from out of the thick brush and running from west to east. "I would like to go down to those flat stones. They are like those near our village, except that ours are yellow like the grasses, while these are red."

"You will have opportunities later to explore this land as much as you desire. But for now we will proceed with your learning." Takoda began to walk along the ridge toward the east, where the ground rose smoothly and no brush grew. It was

late afternoon; the shadows were lengthening; it was very quiet except for the sound of a soft wind rustling in the brush and grasses surrounding the ridge.

"So tell me, Nephew: is that is everything that you are—a bird, an animal, a man, a son, a traveler?"

Tacu thought. "There is nothing else, Uncle. That is what I am."

"Recall then, Nephew, in your vision, what did you see after the hawk caught and killed the father rabbit?"

Tacu thought. "There was a period during which I felt myself to be the air rising high over the land." He looked at Takoda, unsure.

"How can you be the air, Nephew?"

"I know not. I know not what to think about that vision, nor why I felt myself to be the air. I don't think I can be the air, although that is what I saw in my vision."

"Then tell me, Nephew, what is like the air?"

Tacu looked at him, disbelieving. "What do you mean?"

102

"I speak of the nature of things. What things do you know that are like the air?"

"Smoke, Uncle. The mist on the river in the morning, and the fog. And the wavering space above a fire."

"Good. And what else?"

Tacu hesitated. "The spirits that dwell in the East, where my father also dwells?"

"Yes. And do spirits dwell elsewhere than the East, Nephew?"

"Of course, Uncle. They dwell in the plants and bushes, in the antelope who gives us meat and hide, the hawk and the eagle and the *torovim*—our cousin, the porpoise."

"What of your vision, wherein you felt yourself to be the air, and then the newborn rabbit? Did you feel yourself to be a spirit at any time during that vision?"

"I only felt myself to be... myself. When I took the form of the hawk, I could see out of its eyes, which were my eyes. And as the rabbits, I was myself, in their bodies. Even as the air, I only felt like myself...." He mulled it over while Takoda watched him.

"Nephew, open your mind to what is possible. What is it that can take the form of different animals, and also the air itself?"

"Spirit, Uncle. Yes, I must have been a spirit, the spirit that left the body of the dying rabbit." Tacu had a look of wonder on his face. "In my vision, I was a spirit."

"And what about the *Tongva*? Do spirits dwell in the People?"

"I had not thought about that before now, Uncle." He hesitated. "I know that the spirits are about us and guide us. We do not see them, except as animals, the river and other things living. And they may appear to us in visions, but they are not the same as we are." He spoke proudly. "No. We are the People of the Earth."

"What of your father, who dwells in the East. Is he a spirit, he who once was of this Earth?"

"Yes, Uncle, he became a spirit when he left his body to go dwell in the East with the spirits."

"Well then, let me ask you this. When one of the People dies, and his life is gone, what is it that has left that body?"

"It is the spirit of that person, Uncle."

"And if a human is alive, what is it that is present in the body, that is not present when that body is dead?"

Tacu smiled hesitantly. "The spirit of that person, then?"

"Very good. Now consider your experience again, and tell me, what are you?"

"Uncle, in my vision I was the rabbit, then the air, then the newborn rabbit. But I was always felt myself to be only myself, no other." Tacu stopped, focusing on a difficult thought. "As a person, might I be a man, then a spirit alone, then the newborn child like the rabbit?"

"What does your experience tell you?"

Tacu looked at Takoda in sudden understanding. "I was only *one* spirit, even though I felt myself to be the spirit of the hawk, and of the dying and the newborn rabbit. And the air."

"Very good. So then, what are you?"

"I am ... well, I am a spirit."

"Good."

"Uncle, when I was in the air, I could see our bodies far below me, just as we now lie and stand. As though I truly did roam through the air, as spirit." And suddenly, Tacu was certain. He took a deep breath. "Uncle, I see that I am only one thing, I am always *myself.* A spirit. Even as I was the spirit of the hawk and the rabbit, and then the newborn. That was still no other than *myself!*"

Takoda inclined his head in assent.

Tacu continued, speaking rapidly. "It is like the games the young children play, first pretending to be a bear, and another time, a coyote. When one game is finished, they start another right away and continue to play as a different animal." He walked to the edge of the ridge and gazed toward the setting sun, sinking closer to row upon ragged row of blue mountains fading into the distance. "So I am the rabbit, or I am the hawk. Just as our mountain grandfathers there in the distance each have their own character and place. I can be what I want. But now I am a man, to become whom I choose—a hunter, a warrior, a farmer..."

Something else occurred to Tacu and his expression became hopeful and glad. "Or the husband—I can be the husband!" His eyes were shining as he turned back toward Takoda.

Takoda gave him a look of great satisfaction. "Yes, Nephew. Just so." He turned and they began to walk back down the ridge toward the place they had begun. "You now understand your own true nature." After a few more steps he stopped, fixing Tacu with a sharp gaze. "As you live, be what you are as faithfully as you possibly can—take upon yourself all the responsibility of your role willingly. But when it is time for that role to end—accept it with courage and respect for the Creator, and move on to the next."

Tacu nodded, understanding.

Takoda continued. "Just so, when a loved one or a warrior must die, pay them the honor due them, but do not mourn too long. They go on to their next life."

"But my people say that our people who die go to dwell with the spirits in the East...?"

Takoda smiled. "It is not for me to say where a spirit goes when he leaves his body behind. Some

may choose different paths. But the truth I have just taught you is the foundation of your learning. And indeed, the elders of your people also sing of it—they sing, '*As the moon dieth and cometh to light again so we, also having to die, will live again.*'"

Takoda paused to gather his thoughts. "There is one more thing you should realize. While you will learn many new things during the ceremonies at the *Yobangnar,* always trust your own instincts and knowledge above all else. If something does not seem correct, do not feel you must believe it—even if the *Paha* is saying it. Thus will you maintain your own integrity. But question kindly and with respect, if you must question."

Tacu saw the truth in Takoda's words, and nodded slowly.

Takoda gave Tacu a fond look. "Nephew, you have done well. I wish to pay you the respect you are due."

Takoda began chanting a prayer song in an undertone. Moving with ritual care, he took a thong from his belt and deftly tied Tacu's hair into a topknot. Then he carefully removed his own

headdress, lifted it to Tacu's head and fastened it in place. "While you must still seek your initiation with the *Paha* of your village, this day the spirits have indeed seen in you a man, and given you a new name. You shall be called *Wambleesha*, White Eagle. This is a name, like my own, from the Sioux nation. Like your mother before you, you have learned sacred truths about the world, the spirits, and yourself, and like your mother, who became *Panes*, White-headed Eagle Maiden, you have earned the name White Eagle. Your spirit guide has watched over you from the time of your birth. When you fast and partake of the initiation ceremonies, I have no doubt you will see him again."

Tacu recalled his dreams of his father, who watched him as an infant in his mother's arms and then flew away as a great golden eagle. He recalled the crystal and obsidian village, and the eagle guiding him from above to meet with his uncle. Then he saw that Takoda's presence and patience had made all the rest possible. "And you, Uncle, have always been here to guide me, even through my dullness of wit and fears. For this I am grateful."

Takoda gestured in acknowledgement, then began singing again as he unfastened a beautiful elkskin medicine bundle, decorated with otter fur, quills and small animal hides from his belt, and handed it to Tacu. "I bequeath this pouch to you. Its medicine is strong. Teach others what you have learned, so that the wisdom of your people may be spread to your children and their children."

Tacu accepted the pouch with both hands, handling it reverently. He lifted it before him to examine it closely.

"Now, Nephew, it is time for you to return home, to your mother, your village and your maiden. We part company—but only for a time. I go to walk with the spirits for a short while."

Tacu's face reflected shock. "Uncle—you are ill, dying—?"

Takoda shook his head. "No, Nephew. I must go for a time to renew myself, to prepare for another role. I will look in on you from time to time. You will know me again."

Tacu felt a great emptiness settle on his heart and his eyes brimmed with grief. But Takoda

caught his eyes and held them, great kindness and also a wondrous sense of anticipation radiating from him. Despite his sadness, Tacu felt himself lifted and imbued with a powerful sense of peace. In a few moments, like a cloud passing over the land, his grief passed and his expression changed to acceptance and understanding.

From a place just above the sloping ground, he could see the young man's muscled, sweaty back glistening in the orange sunlight as he stood surveying his work. He could see Rómi, looking on, calm and proud, her long white hair flowing like a moonlit waterfall down her back. A young woman stood next to her, her belly just beginning to swell with child. And through their bodies, he could see the outlines of the new sturdy hut, the rows of cultivated sprouts just appearing above the earth, and the bramble and cut tule hedge placed around them to keep them safe from hungry deer. The young man took his young wife's hand gently in his own, then turned and fixed Takoda with piercing black eyes of love as though

Takoda were simply standing on the hill as he always had. Takoda heard him speak to the others.

"He walks, without privation of body or soul, in another world now. He was my vision and my spirit guide. I will know him again." The young man then looked up to the space just above the hill, where Takoda waited. "Go. It is enough."

Takoda turned, satisfied. The deep sky flashed blue around him, and he was in and of the clouds. He would go the way of the eagle, for a time.

ABOUT THE AUTHOR

D.E. LAMONT SPENT HER CHILDHOOD IN THE

blossoming residential developments of the San
Fernando Valley of Southern California in the
1950s and 60s, before the Valley's hilly fringes were
entirely blanketed by expensive homes. She and her

brothers explored the wild chaparral-covered hills and canyons, where they found signs that earlier indigenous people had once lived there. Despite no mention of them in their schoolbooks, these discoveries excited her interest in earlier times and peoples; it was a revelation to her that the fringes of her tract neighborhoods were actually doorways to what in her mind were more natural, and therefore more authentic, worlds.

As an adult, she learned not only that Southern California had been the homeland of the Tongva original peoples for thousands of years, but that around two thousand of their descendents currently lived there. This was shocking to her, because her research had only mentioned an extinct people. To the contrary, she learned that the Tongva community gathers once more—to celebrate their culture and spiritual beliefs, and to protect remaining sacred sites from destruction.

D.E. Lamont wished to honor the Tongva and let more people know about them through her story, which is set in the period just before the encroachment of Spain and the beginning of the

devastation of the Tongva people and culture. By making the story a historical fantasy, she was able to explore the natural methods of practical and spiritual training used by Native Americans, while also creating a hint of hopeful continuity between Tacu's world and the one that was coming—one in which Tacu's people could flourish again.

Another purpose was her wish to show the importance of each individual's self-reliance, independence and ability to act wisely and according to his or her own objectives and sense of honor, without the necessity of seeking the permission of any external human "authority." Tacu learns this in his own world, as modern humankind must also learn in theirs. To give up one's inborn freedoms in the feeble hope of being "taken care of" always has been, and still is, an open invitation to be exploited and enslaved economically and spiritually.

D.E. Lamont is the co-author of three nonfiction books and is working on her first full-length novel. She lives with her husband, two cockatiels and many beautiful plants in a tall

apartment building overlooking the Hudson River in Westchester County, New York. Please visit her website and Journal at www.thewayoftheeagle.com.

ABOUT THE ILLUSTRATOR

JON H. SOEDER IS A TALENTED ARTIST, AUTHOR, and a uniquely gifted individual. His contribution to *The Way of the Eagle* is especially meaningful not only because of the dimension his cover art and beautiful illustrations add, but because of his sensitivity to the natural world and its creatures. Care for and recognition of our oneness with the natural world has always been integral to the life of the indigenous peoples of North America, and it is to Jon as well. His contribution to this book could not be more fitting.

In Jon's autobiographical book, *True Tails*, he shares the never-before-told story of how he discovered at age two that he could "hear" the thoughts of birds and animals—from tiny insects all the way up to the largest creatures living on earth today, the majestic whales—and "speak" back to them with his mind. The book details Jon's coming to terms with his ability and his adventures in doing so, as well as other childhood challenges and triumphs. Its "tails" describe the miracle that is life in all its forms, as the animals' clearly sentient behavior in response to Jon is witnessed by others. Through his book, we gain a understanding of what animals think and feel—about themselves, about life, and even about us. Jon doesn't call himself a "whisperer," but simply a friend of those who inhabit the animal

kingdom. He feels they deserve our admiration and protection.

More of Jon's personal experiences with animals are presented on his website, *The Whale People* (at www.thewhalepeople.com), along with his articles about whales and animal protection issues. Jon is able to clearly present common-sense reasons that gently and rationally support ending the killing of whales and other sentient marine mammals.

Jon lives in Ventura County, California with his family. *True Tails* is available both as a paperback and an ebook.

BIBLIOGRAPHIC NOTE

THE TONGVA LANGUAGE IN THIS BOOK

One of the most important concerns for the Tongva
and those interested in helping to recover and
preserve the Tongva culture is the loss of their
language. The language of a people is in so many

ways the vessel for their unique culture and way of life. Over the several centuries of diminishment and disappearance of the Tongva themselves, their language has likewise been disappearing. At the time I began this story in the mid-1990s, I could only find two books which detailed words for Tongva objects.

Much more recently I found books containing more vocabulary than I had previously found, but the different researchers often reported different words for the same objects or concepts, with no explanation as to the reasons for the differences. Many of those were entirely different from the words I had chosen for my story. These sources also used systems of linguistic notation that would have made reading the words extremely difficult for a nonlinguist.

Finally, I could find no sources of authentic or original Tongva personal names. In lieu of that, I instead used the names of natural objects for the characters, because this is the natural naming system common to many Native American cultures. Therefore, except for a few new words that I added

124

more recently, for the most part I have stuck with the vocabulary I found initially. Since my intention was only to provide readers some examples, as well as the flavor of the Tongva language, and not to provide any kind of exhaustive vocabulary, I felt that what I had found was sufficient for the purpose of this book. The Native American words found in the story, along with several additional words not used in the story, are listed in the glossary following this note.

The good news is that there are linguists, native speakers and others working to recover and restore the Tongvan language and grammar, and teach it to those members of the Tongva nation, and others, who wish to learn. (Please see the website *Keepers of Indigenous Ways, Inc.* at http://www. keepersofindigenousways.org.)

THE TATAVIAM

While my references mentioned the Fernandeño Indians who inhabited the San Fernando Valley, they didn't mention their proper Tongva name, which is "The Tataviam Band of Mission Indians." I

would therefore like to acknowledge the Tataviam, because the Tongva characters in my story were almost certainly part of this band. Their website, *The Fernandeño Tataviam Band of Mission Indians*, tells how their presence in the San Fernando Valley, Santa Clarita Valley and Antelope Valley "... can be traced as far back as 450 A.D. At that time the Tataviam people migrated from the north and settled in villages throughout the area. The villages were constructed on the south-facing sides of hills and mountains because they received the most sun light. The word Tataviam means 'people facing the sun'..." What a beautiful and fitting name for these people! (See their website at www.tataviam-nsn.us/, accessed Nov. 3, 2010.)

REPRESENTATION OF TONGVAN AND BLACKFOOT SPIRITUAL AND RELIGIOUS PRACTICES

Researching the beliefs and culture of the Tongva and the Blackfoot, as practiced and passed on by their respective tribes, has been a profoundly rewarding adventure, and one that I recommend.

I attempted in this book to represent the Tongvan life and culture as faithfully as possible. However, it is important to note that the story I have told is an historical fantasy. The character of Takoda moves through many worlds and, one could say, universes. He brings to Tacu his own knowledge and experience of life, spirit, and truth. What Takoda says and teaches, though inspired by my research, is not intended to be an exact representation of the spiritual beliefs and practices of the Siksika/Blackfoot people.

The following references served as resources for the Native American culture and customs, and for the names of objects and locations used in this book:

- Johnston, Bernice Eastman, *California's Gabrielino Indians* (Los Angeles: Southwest Museum, 1962).

- Mails, Thomas E., *The Mystic Warriors of the Plains* (New York: Barnes & Noble Books, 1995). For information about the Blackfoot and Plains Indians, I relied

upon this amazing masterwork, which contains extremely detailed information about every aspect of Plains Indian life and religion, accompanied by hundreds of beautifully detailed drawings and full-color paintings by the author.

- Miller, Bruce W., *The Gabrielino* (Los Osos, California: Sand River Press, 1991).

- McCawley, William, *The First Angelinos* (Banning, California: Malki Museum Press/Novato, California: Ballena Press, 1996).

- The website *Runajambi – Institute for the Study of Quichua Culture and Health*, for detailed information on Tongva medicinal plants and their names, at www.runajambi.org/tongva/ (accessed Nov. 3, 2010).

GLOSSARY

Tongva Word	Meaning
áman	pestle – "its hand"
Asawtngna	Place of the Eagle – a peak in the Santa Monica Mountains west of Seminole Hot Springs

	and across the grasslands of El Triunfo Canyon – was a well known Tongva landmark resembling a great black eagle with folded wings
ava aha?	How are you?
avakhat	cottonwood tree; boiled pulp used as poultice to help heal wounds
chainoc	I'm unwell
chemeshkwar	acorn meat
crúmi	east
fúmi	north
jungnáa	buzzard
kasili	white sage; has flat, elongated, bluish-lavender leaves
Kawengna	"Place of the Mountain" (origin of the Los Angeles street name Cahuenga)
kich or *ki*	house or hut

kitámi	south
kjot	the whale
kochar	dried currants and gooseberries, used in pemmican
manit	Tongva word for *datura wrightii*; also called "Indian apple," "Jimsonweed," and "nightshade," but is not the same as *Solanum* (the nightshades). Used in religious ceremonies of the Tongva and other tribes; it is a poison, possibly fatal if ingested by humans or animals.
mea!	reply to "I am going"
miyuu	welcome
na-che,	a man
nachochan	a form of greeting in Tongva that means "My eyes see your eyes. My hands are open."
nió-mare!	bless me! (exclamation)

paha	religious chief, village administrator; he instructs the adolescent boys
Panes	a bird feast, during which a girl goes away to the mountains, meets the deity *Chungichnish*, and is transformed by him into the *Panes*, translated as "White-Headed Eagle Maiden." The Tongva believed that the *Panes* was reincarnated each year at this feast.
páymi	west
pemmican	American Indian energy and traveling food, made from dried meat, lard or suet, and dried currants and gooseberries
pinche	body
piwil	great-grandfather (grizzlies are called this)
pul	shaman, or curing doctor, had extensive curing and herbal

knowledge (and supernatural powers: he "possessed 'second sight' and could tell at a glance the moral and physical condition of any person on whom he turned his searching glance"*)

Rómi   Tacu's mother's name, means "North Star"

Siksika   Blackfoot Nation. Includes the Piikani (Piegan) and Kainai (Blood) tribes of southern Alberta, and the Blackfeet of Montana.†

soar   rushes (which grow near water)

Tacu   the son of Rómi; his name means "comet"

---

* Johnston, Bernice Eastman, *California's Gabrielino Indians* (Los Angeles: Southwest Museum, 1962), p. 66

† The website *Siksika* at www.angelfire.com/ar/ waakomimm/sikblf.html (accessed Apr. 21, 2011). Please note that there are slight variances in the different sources' definitions of "Blackfoot Nation," and several other unrelated tribes also use the name "Blackfoot."

takape ahots	bladder pod
Takoda	Tacu's "uncle's" name – a Lakota name meaning "friend to all"
te-gua	the sky
tehépko é	I'm well
tíat	canoe of plank, used by the Tongva peoples who lived on the coastlines of Southern California and who frequented the southern Channel Islands
to-co	animal hide
to-koó-ro't	mountain lion
Tongva	"The People of the Earth" – the name the related native tribes of the Los Angeles basin call themselves; they were referred to by the Spanish settlers as "Gabrielinos" because they lived near the establishment of the San Gabriel mission.

toovit	California brush rabbit
Topangna	"place where mountains run out into the sea" (current name Topanga)
Topangnavit	a native of Topangna
torovim	the porpoise, an intelligent being
Tototngna	"The Place of the Stones" – a Tongva village near the current Chatsworth and West Hills area of the San Fernando Valley; the village nearest Tacu's home
tovangnar	the whole world
tsinitsnits (*plural, tsinitsitsam*)	wise man
wajnuk	seal
Wambleesha	Tacu's adult name, a Sioux name meaning "white eagle"
Wesara	sea gull; Tacu's betrothed's name

wet	oak tree
Wiyot	an animate being in the creation myth said to have died at Big Bear Lake. Also, an old men's song about rebirth, which states: "As the moon dieth and cometh to light again so we, also having to die, will live again."‡
yamu uimi	I am going
Yang-Na or Yabit	Los Angeles
yayare	liar (no male can call his sister this, even in jest)
Yobangnar	large ceremonial shelter or hut where rituals initiating young men into manhood are held
Y-yo-ha-riv-guina	Giver-of-Life, the Creator in Tongva spiritual beliefs

---

‡ Johnston, B.E., *California's Gabrielino Indians*, p. 42.